In Few Words

Ramaswami Mohandoss

ISBN: 0692632395
ISBN-13: 978-0692632390 (Orange Window Publishing)

To my sister, Harini.

Contents

Acknowledgements

If not for the patience and understanding of my wife and daughter, this book would not have happened. Thank you, Sujatha & Pragathi!

I would like to thank my parents and my sister Vidhya for the encouragement I received in all my pursuits.

Thanks to my chief critics, Aneesh Abraham and Vamsee Aluru for helping me find my stories.

My sincere thanks to all my friends who chose to read my stories and share their thoughts: Rameshwar Gowthaman, Sumanth Kumar Gopal, Jayasudha Seenivasan, Malathy Sankaranarayanan, Vijay Raghavan, Esther Kang, Yura Vracko, Venkatramanan Chandrasekhar, and Lijo Joy.

Cover page design: Vijay Raghavan.

A True Story

Today, the speech I've been rehearsing in my bathroom finally finds its stage. To say I'm completely surprised by this would be a blatant lie. Winning this award was never my driving motivation; however, I admit the possible accolades have colored every bit of my work for the past three decades.

Creativity begins with distraction—that divine moment that breaks us out of the surreal and into something real. It marks the very moment an artist is born. The work is work no more but creation, and the outcome becomes a source of inspiration. I was born within that distraction and addicted to it ever since—addicted to inspiring hearts through my work.

The journey wasn't easy. In fact, it took ten long years to get my first significant work before your eyes, but there is no better way to spend one's lifetime than pursuing passion. I started out with neither contacts nor money, watching my ideas get rejected, ridiculed, and even stolen. I have been broke but never short of ideas. I have pure passion for cinema and endless hope. During the toughest times, my love for this medium only grew stronger. There are times when that hope is my only reason to continue, especially when I doubt my own sanity; yet the world is kind enough to watch me persevere and listen to what I have to say.

At this moment, I would like to recognize people from two worlds. The first holds my former acquaintances with whom I had to part ways. I'm sorry; I wish I'd had more patience and been able to convince you of my vision. The second world is made up of my parents; my wife, Jane; and my two children. My parents sacrificed what they had to make sure I had a good education. My wife gave up her career to help me chase my dreams, and my kids sacrificed their dad so the world could get a decent creator. Without you all, I'm not what I am. Thank you.

I wish to dedicate this award to all the families who choose to stand behind every visionary in this world. Thank you, everyone!

Martin read the write-up on his tablet, word for word, for the second time.

The chauffeur navigated the crowded streets, driving Martin and Jane back to their home from the award ceremony.

After observing the traffic through the windows, Martin turned and looked into Jane's eyes for the first time that evening.

Jane was already observing Martin as if patiently waiting for his gaze. She moved closer, dropping her head on his shoulder, and whispered, "Martin, you know in your heart it's not about the award. You gave your best, and you did get nominated. I hope you remember that so you can move onto that next project with your usual zest."

Martin sighed and held her hands, softly playing with her fingertips. He said, "You're right. It was never about the award. I'm not even upset about it being the fifth time either. So what if I have to wait to read my speech again. I've spent all my life trying to inspire others, and nothing is more inspiring than listening to the true story of a fighter. I was only thinking about how the world will have to wait a little more time to hear one such true story."

Sixty-Minute Paradise

I have not been to paradise, but I experience it every day. I stopped using an alarm long ago. My body knows precisely when it's time to wake up. It's four in the morning, and I wake up once again to a beautiful day. Today is also the day before my birthday. Who will send wishes first tomorrow? However hard I try, I cannot evade that question.

I quickly dismiss it one more time to focus on my immediate mission. That first step getting up from my bed is always the most difficult. When the days are cold, it is twice the task. I like to think discipline is the most important quality that an athlete possesses.

I push myself once again and reach for my shoes. I don't recall the last time I missed my early-morning jog. I have a feeling that many, including my family, find my behavior bizarre. They've asked a thousand times why I run, and I keep the answer simple: "I like to run."

I come out of my home, fill my lungs with fresh morning air, and begin my jog.

The road is virtually empty, and the few folks who walk around give me that strange look as I pass them. I have learned to smile and ignore whatever those strangers' perspectives might be. Right now, my focus is to reach that corner street.

It usually takes five minutes to get there at my current speed. The corner street is where I slip out of pain and fall into the zone.

I'm almost there, and I can already feel my heart beating faster than usual. I'm neither worried nor scared, not since the incident a couple of years back when I fainted on the road.

Many tried to discourage me from running alone after that, but I listened to no one. I want to tell everyone that if I can choose my moment to die, it will be while I run. My resolve only got stronger after that incident.

I look around trying to see what has changed since the first day I ran this route. I only have a vague memory of those initial days, but what I observe isn't just a cycle of change. It's more than that. And I'm not just referring to the seasons.

I arrive at that corner, and I slowly fall into that blissful spell full of those precious minutes I spend every day with only me.

After sixty minutes, I arrive at my doorstep one more time, thoroughly rejuvenated—both mind and body.

As I unlock the door, I realize everyone is still asleep. I slowly freshen up and prepare for the rest of the day.

Throughout the day, whatever I do or

wherever I am, the thought of my first birthday wish keeps coming back.

I ignore it until I hit the bed in the evening.

***

It's nine o'clock, and I'm ready for bed. Midnight will be here before I know it, and I have no mission to distract me now. I have no option but to indulge my thoughts and decide my answer.

Who will be the first to wish me a happy birthday tomorrow?

The feeling that it will be Sarah tickles the edges of my consciousness as I yield to my drowsiness.

The next thing I know, I feel a soft tapping. No, it's not my biological clock but Sarah's hands as she gently tries to wake me up.

I open my eyes and see her beautiful face come into focus.

She comes near to my ears and whispers, "Happy birthday!"

I knew it would be her.

I smile a sleepy smile and kiss her forehead. She playfully asks, "OK, how old are you now?" I respond with a wink. "I'm going to let you solve that. In three years, the difference between my age and yours will be zero."

Sarah scrunches her face and looks toward

the ceiling, thinking hard. "Wow! So you will be one hundred years old by the time I turn ten, Grandpa?"

Let Go

Nathan was hoping for a happy ending. It was a Friday morning and also his last day with the company.

A million thoughts ran through his mind while he waited for his meeting with Anderson. His decision to quit and join the competitor wasn't an easy one. His managers and the leaders of the company were clearly not happy to let him go. In the past few weeks, he'd had the opportunity to listen to some interesting promises the company was willing to make in an effort to keep him on board. The offers had been tempting and the conversations delicate. Yet Nathan hadn't relented.

As he waited, Nathan expected to hear another promise from Anderson too.

Anderson was an industry veteran and an inspiration to many. He started his career as a engineer and worked his way up to head the software-engineering division. He didn't meet with every employee who quit.

Nathan knew the reason Anderson wanted to meet him. He was well aware of the unique risk the company faced with him leaving. Nathan had been the brains behind the proprietary demand-forecasting algorithm that was the envy of many in the industry.

Just as Nathan replayed the details of his

career's history, Anderson arrived.

He closed the door, took his seat, and got down to business right away. "So have you made up your mind?" Anderson asked.

Nathan responded slowly and kept his tone formal. "Yes, Anderson. It has been an incredible journey. You have been my inspiration, and I'm thankful to you and everyone in this—"

"Sorry to interrupt. I understand all that. You have been the integral part of the core algorithm we developed..." Anderson stared pointedly at Nathan, allowing him to grasp his boss's line of thought. "We incubated this algorithm in house and have invested heavily on that. It is one of our trade secrets that help us differentiate our services from competition. I'm sure you are aware of all this."

"Yes, Anderson; I understand." Nathan nodded.

"So is there anything that I can do?" Anderson leaned forward slightly, hinting at the possibility of a new counteroffer.

Nathan considered countering but stuck with his original decision. "No, Anderson. I have made up my mind. I hope our path crosses again."

Anderson looked straight into Nathan's eyes for a few seconds, got up to wish him good luck, and left the room.

The meeting had taken less than ten minutes.

Everyone knew Anderson was a no-nonsense person who always did what was right for the company. Anderson fully knew the risk of Nathan leaving for the competition. Yet he'd made no convincing attempt to persuade him to stay. The very act of Anderson letting him go concerned Nathan.

Nathan spent the rest of the day completing his last-day formalities. Then he bid good-bye to the place that had been his second home for the past few years.

***

The following Monday morning, Nathan headed for his new office. He checked his phone for the latest technology news. The first headline got his attention: *In a bold move, Thoughtlet Technologies lets go of its secret sauce.*

Nathan hurried to click the link. He found Anderson's verbatim message as part of the press release. Following the message was a short transcript of the conversation that Anderson had with the press.

After years of incubating and evolving our core demand-forecasting algorithm, we have decided to open it up. The algorithm code is no longer proprietary, and its source code is accessible to everyone on our website.

We are also hosting a contest for every passionate data scientist and developer out there. We invite them to take a look at our code, tinker with it, and make it better. Anyone who can contribute to an improved version of the algorithm will be rewarded in cash!

Press: *It's indeed an interesting move to let go of your important secret sauce. Would you be able to explain the rationale behind such a bold decision?*

Anderson: *In our business, there is hardly a secret sauce that would stay eternal. It's important that we evolve, which would include us proactively outdating our own inventions.*

Press: *How do you think this move would benefit you?*

Anderson: *We are no more bounded by the skill set of our in-house experts. We will benefit from the creativity of a much broader group.*

Press: *With your secret sauce now open in the public domain, are you worried that your competition will now get to know what you had been doing all these days?*

Anderson: *Not at all. Knowing these details would not say much about where we intend to go from* *here. By the way, it is not anyone's secret sauce anymore. From now on, the algorithm can be compared to lettuce.*

Sundar's Dilemma

In that remote town in India, Sundar felt trapped. His evening walk from school had been a peaceful one until he stumbled upon the temptation.

A beautiful red watch abandoned on the road, possibly dropped by some passerby.

Sundar had been yearning for his first watch for quite some time, which only made it all the more impossible to ignore the perfect, bright, shiny timepiece. His heart loved that red watch, but Sundar's mind was yet to resolve the moral dilemma. *Is it right to take that watch and have it for myself?*

He recalled the childhood advice from his mother: "You should never steal."

But this cannot be stealing. The watch was lying there, and he just considered himself lucky enough to stumble upon it.

His father's advice—that opportunity will not come often, and when it does come, one should seize the moment—tripped through his mind, only to be followed by his mother's memorable words: "Never develop an interest in owning things that belong to others. Instead, one should aspire to make or get one's own things."

As he debated his parents' viewpoints in his head, he also recognized one crucial fact: he didn't know the owner of the watch. He had also seen that exact watch in television advertisements multiple times. The road was empty, and nobody was watching. If he picked up the watch and wore it, no one would ever find out.

He was somehow not convinced. Sundar continued to ponder what his mother would have done in such a scenario. She would have either ignored it or reported it to the nearest lost-and-found center, which, in this case, was a nearby police station.

Sundar's friend Ram had a similar watch, and Sundar knew Ram's wasn't expensive. He could not imagine bothering the police over an inexpensive trinket. He was certain they would most likely give up on finding the owner—if they even looked at all.

What if he chose to ignore the watch? Would the person behind him think the same way?

Sundar realized it would take a miracle for the watch to find its owner. Someone else would most likely end up owning that watch. It could be the person walking behind him, or the cop in the police station, or someone who bought it from the cop.

If that was to be the future, why could he not be that new owner?

Just then, Sundar remembered his father's

advice when he'd bought him his first fountain pen: "Sundar, you have got to be careful about your things. You cannot lose them and expect them to come back to you."

The rationale made perfect sense. Probably, the person who dropped this watch was careless and deserved to lose it. By losing it, maybe the person would become more responsible with his other belongings, in the future.

Sundar suddenly felt like a messiah sent by God to teach that careless owner a lesson. Maybe it was God's gift for his birthday coming just next month.

He picked up the watch and vowed never to be careless with any of his stuff.

Sundar's Realization

It was Sundar's most anticipated day of the year, his birthday—his eleventh birthday, to be exact—and in his excitement, Sundar had little trouble waking up early that day.

Like on his previous birthdays, his dad had bought him new clothes. His mom had already prepared his favorite dishes for breakfast and lunch.

Sundar happily sported his new clothes and received his parents' blessing, before leaving for school on his bicycle. He had yet to wear his new watch, though. Sundar hadn't even told his parents about his precious month-old find. He knew his mom would never approve. While he liked the watch a lot, the fact that he'd had to keep it hidden from his parents was something he didn't enjoy a bit.

On his way to school, Sundar placed the watch on his left hand and got ready to flaunt it in front of his friends.

Everyone in class was excited to see his new clothes and his watch.

Sundar was thrilled. He checked the time at least ten times every thirty minutes.

Just before lunch, his excitement grew even higher. His close friend, Shiva, was joining him for lunch from another class, and Sundar couldn't wait to show off his new watch. Sundar decided to share the truth about the watch with his best friend.

As soon as the lunch bell rang and Sundar stepped out of his class, Shiva came running toward him and gave him a tight hug.

"Happy birthday, Sundar!" Shiva's voice was full of sincerity.

"Thanks. How are my new clothes?" Sundar asked eagerly, looking into his friend's eyes.

"They're very nice. Could I have the sweets your mom made?" Shiva grinned.

"Absolutely!" Sundar slowly brought up the topic as he shared the sweets. "And do you like my new watch?"

Shiva hummed and savored the sweets before taking a close look at the watch. "Wow! It's nice too. You mentioned your dad giving you a watch if you performed well in exams, right? Did your dad surprise you on your birthday instead?"

Sundar shifted in his seat, uncomfortably admitting the truth for the first time. "No. I actually found it on the road a month back while I was walking home."

"Oh! It's not yours, then?" Shiva's focus had shifted fully to the sweets.

They shared their lunch, enjoyed a friendly chat, and left for their classes at the bell.

***

On his way home, Sundar reminisced about his day but, more importantly, thought about his watch. While he loved the watch, for some reason, Sundar wasn't fully happy wearing it.

He looked at his shoes and remembered the moment his dad gifted them after Sundar had scored the highest grade on his exams. He also recalled doing well in a sports event and being gifted his bicycle. The happiness and pride that he experienced every time he touched them was clearly missing when it came to the watch.

As he reflected on those memories, Sundar got distracted by the sound of the temple bell ringing nearby.

He parked his bicycle outside, walked inside the temple, and found a donation box. He heard his mom's voice as clearly as the day she spoke the words while dropping some money into it.

"Whatever one puts in this box will be used to do something good."

Without a second thought, Sundar removed his watch and slipped it into the donation box.

As he pedaled home in the pleasant evening breeze, Sundar realized he was finally filled with the happiness and pride that had been eluding him since morning.

Recognizing a Hero

"**P**aul has a strange sense of humor. At times, it's hard to know his intent until the conversation is fully over." Frank observed the audience indulge in familiar, knowing smiles. "On a serious note, Paul is a pillar of our organization and truly deserving of this award. More than the award, however, I'm personally thrilled that everyone recognizes his contributions." Frank, VP of the department and Paul's super boss, gestured toward the guest of honor seated in the first row.

Sitting next to him was the man who had been his manager since he had joined the company two decades ago: Wayne. They'd worked together on many critical projects over the years and had succeeded in most. However, Wayne had never appreciated Paul wholeheartedly, even once, and it had become more than a growing concern for Paul.

"To give one's best, consistently, for over twenty years, is something remarkable. I've had the opportunity to work with Paul directly on some of the critical projects, and I thoroughly enjoyed it every time. I'm happy that he chooses to be with our organization. Thank you, Paul, and I wish you nothing but the best in your career." Frank stepped from the stage to a roar of applause as the function headed to its final episode, which was a speech by Paul himself.

Paul stood and shook his hands with Frank.

He stood onstage and, once the applause settled down, smiled at the happy faces of his friends, family, and colleagues. "This is a very special moment. Having spent over twenty years in my career, I fully realize the importance of recognition. Recognizing someone's effort adds meaning to his or her pursuit, especially during tough times. I understand how difficult it can get to recognize and appreciate someone's effort just at the right time, before it can become late." Saying that, Paul made a subtle glance at Wayne before continuing with his speech. "Quite early in my career, I realized something important—best effort has little to do with the best outcome. A little ironic, maybe, but that's the hard truth. Does that mean one stops giving his best effort? No. If one wants to create that best-outcome opportunity, there's no option but to put the best effort in every moment."

Thunderous applause exploded, especially from the leaders of his organization who nodded their head in unison.

"So many nice things were said about me here today. I'm not sure how true all of them are, but I'm humbled by your recognition, affection, and kindness. I would like to answer any questions that you might have for me."

Paul watched one of his close friends and colleagues reach for the microphone.

"In one word, how exactly do you feel at this moment?"

"Blessed."

Smiles sprinkled across the faces of several audience members.

Paul watched Sam, another colleague of his, reach for the microphone.

"It is certainly the biggest recognition that the company has for its employees. Of course, there are a lot of people who have helped you get here. If you had to attribute this success to one person, who would it be?"

Paul saw many eyes rest on Wayne. Paul lapsed into even deeper thought but came back quickly. "Robert Smith," he said, leaving everyone in the crowd shocked and confused. Wayne, however, remained as cool as ever.

Sam tilted his head. "Robert Smith? Did you work with him?"

"No."

Sam turned to face the others in the audience. When he received nothing but shrugs and head shakes in return, he faced Paul once again. "Was he here in this group?"

"No. He left the company nineteen years

back."

"Wait. What?" Sam scratched his head. "He left nineteen years ago? Are you in touch with him?"

Paul chuckled softly and shook his head. "Nope. I have never even spoken to him."

"You must be joking!" Sam threw his hands in the air, huffing in frustration.

Paul, with his usual strange smile, said, "Twenty years back, when I was fresh out of college and training, I was clueless and confused about where my career was headed. I got this call from Cindy, my HR contact, about my first project. When we met, Cindy took me to the office of Robert Smith. Bob, as he was better known, was managing the testing team then and running late. We waited for several minutes, and when Bob still didn't show, Cindy decided to introduce me to the manager of the engineering division instead, so my trip wasn't a complete waste.

"I attribute this moment to Bob. His busy schedule and inability to meet that day created the opportunity for me to work with one of the finest leaders in this company for the next twenty years."

Paul paused and looked into Wayne's eyes. "Thank you, Wayne."

A Thankless Job

I sometimes wonder—what's the point? Why should I care so much about moving stuff from one end to the other? What have I gotten in return for the tireless effort I put forth day in and day out for months and even years? Forget recognition—unless something goes wrong, I don't even get noticed. What's the point of being on a pedestal when nobody really sees you? To find a moment of peace, I need to either slow things down or mess things up. And every time I do, I get only a short breather before I'm plugged back into the routine.

Am I taken for granted? Be it their education or entertainment, I am the family's lynchpin, yet I can't avoid the idea of it all being a thankless job.

Nobody cares if I even need a bath.

There were many instances in the past when strangers approached me, wanting to connect, and I rejected their advances without a thought in an effort to remain fully faithful and available to this family.

Sometimes I wish I could walk away from this house.

It hurts when some of the family, particularly the little ones, don't have any concept of the value and joy I bring to their lives, when they stare at me as if I'm some jerk who can only blink.

Apart from the pain, there are certain things I enjoy, too. For instance, nothing that happens in this family escapes my notice for long. Almost everyone inevitably shares his or her secrets with me. Be it Eric's work-related stuff or Maya's projects, I know everything going on in their lives.

My second-biggest joy comes in getting acquainted with new friends. There was nothing quite like a legitimate friend in search of a long-term relationship. It's been a while since I've experienced that joy. My last encounter happened when Maya brought him home for the first time. He was cute, short, and black in color.

Today has been a relatively quiet day, as both Eric and Maya have been away most of the evening.

But now I notice Eric entering the house with Maya and carrying a beautiful box. The box has a picture of an apple with a bite taken out of it.

I remember a similar box around when I first met my last friend.

Maya opens the box, and to my absolute delight, I watch her welcome someone resembling my last acquaintance. This new guy looks older, though.

Maya checks with Eric for some information and, after receiving it, begins working with this guy.

Just as she finishes, I experience that moment I've been waiting for a long time. Yes, a new acquaintance has arrived with a legitimate access key, seeking a long-term relationship.

I fully embrace the new member and add him to my network.

The moment I do, I see that smile on Maya's face.

I once again stand tall and happy, proudly plugged in to that familiar routine I do so well: securely routing bits of data, one after another and another and another...

The Perfect Hire

While most scrambled around the periphery for evidence, Matt quickly judged someone through a few seemingly innocuous questions.

There was an instance when Matt had to interview a candidate by name Pete. Though Pete came with a strong recommendation from his boss, who also happened to be Matt's colleague, Matt remained skeptical. Matt knew Pete's boss would only collaborate for his own benefit.

During interview, while the remaining panelists desperately tried to make sense of Pete's capability, Matt, with a single question, expertly ended the interview.

"Who initiated the conversation concerning your movement to my team? Was it you or your boss?"

In that instance, it was his boss.

Pete stayed with his old boss, only to be laid off the very next month for poor performance.

Today, an afternoon interview is scheduled with a man named Jack to fill an important position that has been open for a while.

Matt already has his questions ready.

***

On the other end of the city, Jack sighs and rolls off his couch simply because he can't sleep anymore. He had hit the couch around seven the previous night and lay there for more than fifteen hours before remembering his interview that afternoon.

He reluctantly moves to the bathroom, only to settle down on his couch again with a bowl of cereal.

Realizing he has a few more hours before his interview, he picks up the remote control and clicks a button, starting the DVD player. He can't remember the last movie he watched, but he's too lazy to get up and check.

He waits in hopeful anticipation for the opening credits of his favorite movie, *Psycho,* but gets *Sleepless in Seattle* instead. Jack is positive this is the work of his girlfriend, Jesse.

He's seen this movie at least forty times. Each time he watches it, he only hates it more, especially when he finds Jesse crying at the very end...every time.

Once again, he takes a deep breath and, in an attempt to conserve energy, sits back, making the hard decision to watch the movie for the forty-first time.

About halfway through the movie, Jack feels a sudden sense of urgency and realizes if he doesn't expend the effort to get off the couch, he will very likely be late for his interview.

He showers quickly and rushes to get

dressed. Only once he is midway through the downtown commute does Jack glance at his watch. He's at least forty-five minutes out, which means he's at least fifteen minutes late.

He speeds along the freeway and makes it to the building just after two o'clock.

As he runs through the main lobby, he scans the directory and finds the office he needs is on the tenth floor.

He reaches the elevators, and disaster strikes hard in the form of a message: *Elevators temporarily out of order.*

Jack had not expected a ten-floor hike. He is about to give up but decides to take the stairs. By the time he reaches the office, it is 2:15 p.m.

Jack apologizes to the receptionist for his delay and mentions his appointment.

She quickly checks the list and informs him that Matt was scheduled to meet with someone else at two o'clock.

For a moment, Jack wonders how he screwed this up too. Did he come to the wrong office, or was his interview scheduled for a different date? It wouldn't surprise him, after all. He has never been a details man.

He clears his throat and requests she check Matt's other appointments for the day.

She checks the calendar and states, "Yes, you

do have an interview with Matt today. But it's at three, not two."

Jack sighs with relief and heads toward the couch in the reception area to wait patiently.

***

At 3:00 p.m. sharp, Matt walks out to welcome Jack, taking note of the man's body language.

Matt sets the discussion's tone with three simple questions to judge Jack's capabilities and level of honesty from the outset.

"Do you like watching movies?"

Jack stares at Matt for several seconds but answers the question without batting an eyelash. "Yes."

Simple. Straightforward. "What movie have you watched the most?"

"*Sleepless in Seattle.*"

"What time did you reach our office?" Matt watches every movement Jack makes, looking for telltale signs.

"Two ten."

No change in breathing. No shifting in his seat. Matt nods almost imperceptibly and asks his final question. "How did you reach this floor? Did you take the stairs or the elevator?"

Jack glances toward the stairwell door and chuckles softly. "I took the stairs."

Matt jots some notes on the tablet in front of

him, and by 4:00 p.m. the recruiter has them in hand.

Jack is a capable candidate. Very sociable, demonstrates empathy, a great planner, and a hardworking guy. He is a must-hire!

To Tell the Truth

For the past two weeks, Emma hadn't asked for her favorite candy. She hadn't shown an interest in playing with her friends either. It was beginning to concern Lisa. She had never seen her five-year-old daughter behave like that before.

It all started when Emma visited her grandpa's house a couple of weeks back. Everything was fine until Emma noticed her grandma's empty room. Her grandma had been unwell for a year and passed away the previous month. Emma wasn't informed of her death, and her only question since then had been about where her grandma had gone

Lisa tried to evade the question, thinking her daughter would forget. However, in the past two weeks, Emma only became more and more curious. The thought of someone suddenly vanishing from her world without a plausible explanation clearly disturbed Emma every day.

That day, Lisa knew, just by looking into her eyes when she picked her up from school, that Emma was not happy. She realized that a delicate conversation about death had become inevitable.

Lisa decided tonight was the night, and she waited for Emma to initiate the topic.

Emma would normally ask her mom about her grandma after dinner. That evening was no different.

"Where did Grandma go?"

Lisa kept her tone soft and even as she jumped into the conversation she'd been dreading. "She left us to stay at a different place."

Emma faced her mom with a determined gaze. "Why? Couldn't she live with us?"

"Grandma died, sweetheart, so she can't live with us anymore." As she answered, Lisa prepared herself to answer even more delicate questions. She glanced at Michael, who continued to remain engrossed in work on his laptop.

Emma gnawed her bottom lip, lost in thought, and asked, "Why did she die?"

"She died because she grew very old."

"So will everyone die when they grow very old?"

Lisa took a deep breath and answered the question honestly. "Yes, Emma."

"Will you die when you grow very old?" Emma looked into her mother's eyes.

Lisa sensed where the conversation was going. Emma's eyes were already wet with unshed tears. Lisa smiled, held her daughter's cheeks, and replied, "Yes, dear. But that's many years away. Mom and Dad are very healthy and will spend a long time with you."

Emma reached out, picking at the seam of her mom's jeans. "Can we go and meet Grandma?"

Lisa shook her head. "No, Emma. That is not possible."

"Why?"

Lisa brushed her fingers through Emma's soft hair. "Only Grandma knows her new place."

"How did Grandma go to her new place? Did she have to walk?"

"When Grandma died, we dressed her in her nice clothes and left her alone so God could help her find the path."

"Could we ask God to tell us where Grandma is?"

Lisa nodded. "Yes, we can. God has answers for us when he decides to share them. Anyway, God will take good care of Grandma."

Though Emma wasn't crying yet, Lisa saw her daughter wasn't convinced.

"Will her new place be as safe as our home?"

"Yes."

Emma stared at her mother and frowned, looking for incontrovertible proof the way only a five-year-old can. "How do you know that? We can't see God or that place, so how do we know that Grandma will be safe there?"

Lisa found it difficult to answer that

question.

Emma's little chin quivered as the tears finally started to fall. "I'm scared. I'm scared of what will happen to Grandma and all of us after we die."

Unable to console her, Lisa looked desperately at Michael.

***

Michael closed his laptop, pushed it aside, and asked Emma to come sit next to him. He gave her a hug and wiped her tears. He then slipped her tiny hand in his and walked toward the patio.

Michael noticed the garden pots that Emma used to water every day. Five sunflowers of different sizes, which had blossomed the previous day, smiled at him. "Look at these flowers. Aren't these beautiful? Did you water the plants today, dear?"

After a brief silence, Emma touched the edge of one pot. "Yes, I did."

"It looks like the flowers are smiling at us, doesn't it?"

Emma nodded. "Yes. They all look happy."

"Do you know where these sunflowers came from?"

Emma looked confused. "These are here, in our house."

Michael smiled and nodded. "You are right,

Emma. These sunflowers did blossom here, in our house. But do you remember how it all began?"

Emma looked at each plant and then back at her father. "We put one seed in each pot, and I watered them every day after that."

Michael squatted beside his little girl and placed a hand on her shoulder. "Yes, it all started from a seed. The seed grew into a stem, which then sprouted a leaf, and then..."

"And then this flower."

Michael clapped his hands and grinned at Emma. "Do you know where those seeds came from?"

Emma shook her head but appeared curious.

"The seeds you put in these pots actually came from another sunflower that grew in some farm at a place far away from our home."

Emma gasped. She glanced at the closest flower and asked, "So the sunflowers we have are the same sunflower that grew on that farm?"

Michael nodded. "Yes. The sunflower, after growing old at the farm, came to our home as those seeds."

"How did those seeds reach our house?"

This time, Michael spoke slowly and clearly. "It's the work of God. He ensured the seeds arrived at the shop in a box, safe. Daddy bought those seeds and brought them home for you to grow into beautiful, smiling sunflowers." After a few moments, Michael said, "Just like those seeds, after we die, God will find us a new place—a place where we will continue to grow, smile, and live a happy life, just like these sunflowers."

Soul Mate

J im was thrilled and could not wait. He was one of the few elite members chosen by his company to attend a prestigious technology conference. Jim believed he had truly earned the trip to Las Vegas, along with two of his colleagues. In Vegas, he was set to speak about his company's perspective on what the technological future looked like. Ever since the news broke, Jim had been walking a few inches off the ground.

That evening, he left work early and headed home to share the good news with Kate. His wife never had any interest in technology or gadgets, but she was someone with a remarkable intellect and presence of mind.

Jim parked his car and realized he had forgotten his keys again. Staying inside his car, he texted his wife from the garage to let her know he had arrived.

As Jim picked up his bag from the car, Kate opened the door and said, "Forgot the keys once again? Maybe it's time for me to act on your forgetfulness."

Jim smiled and entered the house.

After tossing his bag on the couch, Jim began looking for something in the refrigerator, while Kate grabbed the watering can from the counter.

Jim settled on the couch with a loud sigh and

a drink. "Guess what, honey? I've made it to the elite group. Three of us are leaving for Vegas tomorrow morning for the conference. I'm the keynote speaker sharing our company's take on the industry's future."

"That's good." Kate continued watering the plants.

"That's *good*." Jim was not pleased with her response. "Is that it?"

"Yeah, it's only a point of view about the future, right? You will get the response that you expected when you actually build that future." Kate winked.

"Hmm." Jim took a quick look at the time on his cell phone. It was already eight o'clock.

A slight shiver rippled down his spine as he was reminded of his early-morning flight. He was not an early riser. He knew that to make the six o'clock flight, he had to wake up at four and reach the airport before five. "Honey, I've got to wake up at four tomorrow. Please don't let me oversleep tomorrow morning."

"OK. Make sure you set your alarm right and your phone isn't in silent mode."

After dinner, Jim packed his bag and hit the hay early, while Kate cleared things in the kitchen. He set his alarm for four the next morning, ensured the phone was not on silent mode, and went to sleep.

***

Jim woke to the alarm and, with great difficulty, pried open his eyes to observe the time. He did quick math and thought he could still make it, even if he snoozed for ten more minutes.

The next thing he remembered, he was staring at the glowing five on his phone's clock. He had overslept once again.

He rushed around the room, getting ready in ten minutes. As he picked up his wallet, he found Kate had printed his boarding pass. Thanking her in his mind, he reached for his keys. He looked at the time on the cell phone—5:15 a.m. He had forty-five minutes to make the flight.

Just as he started the ignition, he got a call from Kate. He decided to call her back from the airport to save that precious minute.

Jim took the expressway, and luckily, the traffic was light.

He reached the airport and checked the time once more—5:35 a.m. Since he didn't have any checked baggage and his boarding pass was already printed, he headed directly to the security gate.

He received another call from Kate, which he once again ignored.

He cleared security and strode toward the gate, dialing Kate's number as he hurried through the terminal.

As soon as she picked up, he spoke. "Honey, I'm rushing to the boarding gate as we speak. I'm in a hurry. I overslept again. I just have ten minutes before the flight takes off. Not sure if the boarding gate is already closed. Will talk to you in detail once I reach Vegas. Love you."

Kate responded slowly yet clearly. "Dear, don't panic, and listen to me carefully. I was pretty sure you would do all this. That's why, after you went to sleep last night, I went online, printed out your boarding pass, and changed the time on your phone. It's a quarter to five. You have plenty of time for the flight. Don't forget to reset the clock on your phone. Good luck!"

Fallen in Love

Talking in my mind, or talking to you, while I'm alone is not new to me. It is something I thoroughly enjoy.

Today is a very important day. What lies in front of me is likely to be the slowest ten minutes I'll ever go through—the time I have to spend with myself before you arrive.

Last night, I decided not to delay this any further. Come what may, I'm going to open my heart and let you know how I feel. That's why I texted you, citing a work emergency, and suggested we meet today at this restaurant.

"Are you ready?"

The waiter brings me back to reality.

I let the waiter know I'm waiting for someone special and will need more time. I then notice the second hand slow to a crawl on my watch and decide to get back to reminiscing of the past two years, especially the moment when it all started.

When did I see you first? It was in that team-building session we had at work. It was your first week on the job, and while the entire team was having fun in the park, I saw you riding that swing all by yourself. That moment, with just your smile, I knew something about you was going to remain in me forever.

In my world, love at first sight was a joke

until then. I never imagined a smile could make me feel so vulnerable. Every time I indulge in your smile, I feel guilty. I didn't want to believe it, but I'm hopelessly aware that I'm addicted to you now.

I feel that veil of arrogance melt every time you look into my eyes. Every moment you are close to me, I fear I might lose it all. I fear I might become a child again. Yet I feel happy if that means I get you.

I can't help wondering—if you hadn't been part of my team, would I have ever gotten the courage to even talk to you?

Reality suddenly strikes again, and I feel my heart grow heavy. I feel that usual anxiety taking over. What if all these sweet memories turn bittersweet once you arrive? Will your *no* completely take you out of my world?

Why think like this now?

I've been considering this for almost two years.

I take a quick look at my watch to see I have that final minute to wait.

As the clock hits ten, I hear the door swing open behind me.

I turn around to see my beloved come in with that subtle smile—the smile that is invisible to almost everyone but brilliant enough to keep me completely hooked for over two years.

"Excuse me, young lady, are you ready to order now?"

I ask the waiter to give me one more minute and turn toward the entrance once again. I stand up, give him a hug, and look into his eyes, ready to begin the most important conversation in my life.

An Unseen
Accomplishment

It had rained incessantly ever since Sathya got back from school. Born and raised in Mumbai, he was barely disturbed by the monsoon weather. Even on a sunny day, Sathya wouldn't miss playing with his friends, and today, he was engrossed for over three hours in a puzzle. His dad was away for work, and he had already resolved to solve that puzzle before he arrived home for dinner.

He had received the puzzle in the form of a small peculiar statue. The statue was made of stone, and no matter which side he looked at it, he was unable to make any sense of what it was.

Sathya started from scratch, observing three significant parts of the statue. The first was a small stick, flat on one side and a little curved on the other. At the bottom of the stick, he found something resembling a pair of hands. The second part was a protruding tube with flaps on either side. The tube tapered and curved toward the edge too. The third significant piece was flat, possibly the base of the statue. Above the base looked to be a pair of legs, bent at the knees. It seemed as if someone was taking position to begin their run.

What could that tapered tube be? It was definitely not a water tube. Could it be the trunk of an elephant? Yes, every detail on and around that tapered tube resembled the trunk of an elephant.

With that, Sathya could see the pieces fitting together. The two flaps on either side were the elephant's ears.

But an elephant would have four legs, and the statue just had two.

What kind of elephant had only two legs? Could it be Lord Ganesh, then? Yes, it was very possible. *Ganesh, the Hindu god of all new beginnings*, does have an elephant face and a human body.

Sathya was feeling confident after putting two of the three pieces together.

If it was Lord Ganesh, what was that stick in his hands? The Ganesh he was aware of didn't hold anything.

Sathya decided to focus only on that flat stick. He tried to recall all the objects that he knew of that resembled a stick. The first thing that came to mind was a cricket bat. That fit neatly into what he had observed so far.

But why would Ganesh, a Hindu god, hold a cricket bat in his hands? It didn't make much sense to Sathya.

Just as he was about to reject that notion, he recalled his visit to the market with his dad one Sunday. His dad was explaining the numerous

Ganesh idols displayed for the upcoming festival. He remembered his dad even mentioned a Spider-Man Ganesh.

Sathya felt a eureka moment. He was holding a statue of Lord Ganesh playing a cricketing shot. Fully satisfied, Sathya stood, picked up his *white cane*, and guided himself slowly toward the living room. He couldn't wait to hear the doorbell ring and share his moment of accomplishment with his dad.

A Big Heart

It was Saturday morning, and Sean woke up to a typical day. Except for the party in that evening, his day was filled with routine tasks. He had yet to confirm his attendance at the party, though.

The party was to celebrate the success of a recently released movie that had just bombed in the box office. Sean played a small character role in that movie. While he hated these types of parties, Sean had always attended them in the past. Apart from helping him to get in touch with potential influencers of the future, the parties kept him visible in the circle.

He looked at the list of attendees to see if anyone could inspire him. He found a confirmation from Robin that made him pause.

Sean related a lot to Robin's past. Like Sean, Robin had also been a college dropout, genuine artist, and someone who struggled for over ten years to make it. The only difference was that Robin finally got his break last year. He was the lead protagonist in his last movie, which turned out to be a blockbuster. It was an offbeat movie, and his character was a quirky and a difficult one, just that kind of role that Sean had always yearned to play. While Sean had played similar roles in the past, this character was etched to perfection, and Robin pulled it of remarkably.

Seeing that confirmation, Sean decided to attend the party. After taking care of that decision for the day, Sean chose to stay in the bed and laze about with nothing but his past.

Ten years had passed since Sean left school for his chance to make it big in the movies. Over the years, he had done all kinds of work and relentlessly acquired many skills. He had yet to get that right opportunity to showcase them all. Like every passionate artist, he continued to work hard and wait patiently for his luck to turn.

That evening, Sean sported his best suit. He knew surviving in a world of glitter meant it was all about the packaging. He was aware that the party would most likely be filled with pseudo celebrities—celebrities created by the media for its own survival.

The party was attended by wannabe movie stars and those faded stars of the past. He attempted to strike up conversations with budding directors and looked forward to dinner.

Just as his interest level was sinking to its lowest point, he felt a tap on his shoulder. He looked back and found none other than Robin grinning back at him.

"How are you, Sean?" Robin, unlike everyone else who had asked, sounded genuinely interested in his answer.

"I'm doing fine, Robin. How about you?" Sean shook hands with Robin, reciprocating the same level of sincerity. "That last performance you gave was splendid. I thoroughly loved your character. I hope I get to play that kind of a character sometime. I didn't think I'd get an opportunity to congratulate you in person."

Robin looked less than excited hearing that. "Got to tell you something, Sean."

"Sure. What's up, Robin?"

Meeting Sean's gaze, Robin said, "Frank, who wrote the script for that movie, is a close friend of mine. His original thought was to have you play that character. He revealed that little secret when he wanted to get my perspective on his work. I liked the script a lot and convinced him to let me play that character instead." Robin shifted from one foot to the other and then touched Sean's shoulder. "Wanted you to be aware of the truth."

With that, Robin turned and walked away.

Sean stood still, trying hard to decide if what he'd heard was for real. His heart began to beat faster, and the two glasses of water he gulped provided little help.

Sean felt his world had come to an end. Robin had not stolen his opportunity but his future. He stepped out of the party hall and had a sudden craving for a cigarette.

He rushed to a nearby store. As he picked up his pack of cigarettes, he felt an overwhelming sense of cruelty.

As he inhaled his first puff, he realized a hatred for Robin was brewing somewhere deep in his heart.

He began to cough, which intensified that growing hatred with every puff. Of course, this was his first cigarette in ten years.

"How could he do that to me?" He fully knew that the question, along with its answer, was completely futile. For a brief moment, he even indulged in the idea of ending Robin's life. Before he decided to hate Robin forever, a random thought occurred to him. "What would I have done if I had been in Robin's position? Would I have let go of the opportunity?" With that question, his hatred suddenly seemed to have lost its purpose. In that moment of distraction, Sean found clarity.

He dropped his half-smoked cigarette and stamped it out. He took a deep breath of fresh air, put a smile on his face, and vowed to never smoke again. Trashing the rest of the pack, Sean began the walk back to the party hall.

A Renewed Partnership

Except for a one-on-one trust they had in each other, Lee and John were poles apart. Be it their vision, conviction, or their talents, they were completely different. If Lee was about depth in a subject, John was all about breadth. If Lee was a shrewd investor, John would have been a master speculator. In essence, Lee was a great doer, and John was a great seller. They shared a complex relationship. While they hardly spoke to each other, they did admire each other. After all, there was no way this partnership would have survived the test of time. They fully knew their skills and talent conflicted head on; they also knew their strength was in staying together for one purpose.

Their partnership began a year ago, when Lee came up with a brilliant idea and convinced John of its potential. The idea had all the potential to be the next Google or Facebook. Lee spent the entire year building the idea into a product, and John funded the whole thing. Their partnership would be a success only when they completed that last lap together.

Together, they had to find that investor who would take the product to market. Here was where their partnership felt the biggest strain.

John had already found four potential investors, but all of them wanted the product to be tweaked a bit so that it could make immediate money through advertising.

Lee was completely against it. He believed it would make the customers repulsive to the product. He would ask, "How much do you enjoy ads while watching your favorite movie?"

John was unable to convince Lee or the investors. With everything at stake, John was showing signs of frustration.

John had a meeting planned with the fifth potential investor for Monday, but there were already rumbles of the same demand.

If they lost that investor too, it would most likely end it all. He had to convince Lee to relent and agree to the investor's terms before the meeting.

***

Monday morning, Lee woke to a knock on the door. He couldn't figure out who would stop by at five in the morning.

He opened his door to discover nobody on the other side.

Finding it weird, he locked the door and returned to his bed, only to hear the doorbell ring.

Once again, an empty doorstep awaited him, so he decided to take a stroll around his house.

To his surprise, he found John standing on the side of his home.

John had never come to his home that early, ever.

Noting his partner's pensive mood, Lee knew John had come to discuss something very important.

He called John inside, offered him coffee, and waited for the conversation to start.

John took a sip and met Lee's gaze. "This fall will be one year since we started our hunt for an investor. The investor we're meeting today is likely to be the last potential investor we'll talk to. He is likely to ask for the same change the others asked for." John took another sip and set his cup on the counter. "By now, everybody is aware that you built a great product. So even if we fail here, you're sure to get a job anywhere you want and have a secure future. That's not the case with me. I bet everything on this, including my house."

Lee listened and then took a deep breath. "So...what do you want me to do?"

"I know your conviction, but you have got to relent."

"I understand, John. Let me take a shower and meet you at your place in a couple of hours." Lee stood and gestured toward the door. "Now try to relax and head home."

After an hour, Lee arrived at John's house to pick him up. They both remained silent during the entire journey.

After twenty minutes, John looked around, surprised, as they arrived at the office of Morgan, their legal advisor. "Why are we here, Lee?"

"Please. Just hold on. I'll explain." Lee ushered John inside. He asked Morgan, "Do we have them all ready?"

Morgan glanced at both of them and nodded. "Yes, Lee."

"Great. Can I have those?"

Morgan handed Lee a file filled with paperwork, and Lee proceeded to sign every page of it.

John assumed it was some contract but was unable to see any details. "What are we doing here, Lee?"

Lee didn't respond until he completed his signature on the last page. He then looked straight into John's eyes. "John, in the best interest of our business, I have to be honest. I'm not going to change my stance, and I still believe we will win this together if we don't relent. You mentioned that regardless of how today's meeting goes, my future is secure. Here is my signed copy of an empty contract. In the event of us failing and me succeeding elsewhere alone, you are entitled to have whatever you think that secure future is."

John picked up the file and found Lee's signature on ten blank sheets of paper.

A Reflective Moment

Noel and Leon seldom reached a consensus when they talked, yet Noel met Leon every day and discussed his key issues, especially those touching on morals and ethics. Though Noel had disagreed to many of his suggestions, Leon never refused to meet Noel.

That day, Noel prepared for one such meeting. He was about to move forward with a decision that concerned his wife. Noel knew his discussion with Leon was not going to be an easy one.

Leon walked in and started without missing a beat. "So you have decided to kill her."

"No! I would not call it *killing*."

"OK." Leon huffed and crossed his arms. "You have decided to end her life, right?"

"I wouldn't call it that either. She has been suffering for the past several years. I'm only trying to relieve her misery."

Leon shook his head. "No, Noel. You are choosing words that suit your convenience. While it's true Jen has been in a coma all these years, it's *your* perception that she's suffering or in misery. She never told you about her suffering, right?"

Noel sighed. "No, she did not tell me. But I know it."

"You know it? How?"

"Be-because it's the truth."

Noticing the stutter, Leon took a deep breath but continued pushing his point. "Come on, Noel. You call your opinion of Jen a truth? Explain that to me."

Noel was getting uncomfortable and evaded any eye contact with Leon. "She is in an irreversible comatose state. You are aware of that. As per the doctors, no other patient who entered that state has ever returned."

"Are you saying Jen will never regain consciousness?"

"None have ever come back." Noel tried to avoid directly answering the question. "Any doctor would agree."

"You said no one regained consciousness, but my question is simple—do you know for sure that Jen will not wake up?"

Noel, his head down, spoke softly. "No."

"Which means you are not completely aware of the truth. Without knowing the truth, how can you decide to end somebody's life?"

After a few moments of silence, with tears in his eyes, Noel asked, "What is the value in existing in that state of limbo?"

Leon heard him out before he spoke. "Isn't Jen the best person to decide that? We don't know her decision yet. How does all this hurt you, Noel? Is it because she is your responsibility and you don't want to take care of her anymore?"

"Yes, I have grown tired looking after her. In fact, it started twenty years back when she fell into a coma. Back then, I did not think I would end up living my life with only hope. That hope is no more within me. Be it my career or life, I doubt if I have anything else to give. With my hope fully gone, I'm unable to imagine her get up and walk. Seeing her lying in the bed with eyes closed, day after day, I have started to wonder if there would even be a difference." Noel completely broke down and began crying.

Leon decided not to push any further and allowed Noel to get through his emotion.

After a few minutes, Noel collected himself, bid Leon good-bye by clearing the vapor off the mirror, and walked out of the bathroom.

Like a Tulip

She could have asked for that kiss
But chose to speak through her eyes instead
I could have given it right then
Yet decided to remember the moment forever

Vaughn placed his pen in his journal and looked around the crowded bus. He could have heard a pin drop.

Fifty other men in fatigues and uniforms were on their way to the naval station in Everett. From there, they would begin their long journey to various military bases overseas.

Vaughn had arrived two weeks earlier for a month-long vacation but cut it short to respond to a critical mission. While Vaughn was holding his heart strong, he was unsure how long he would be able to continue.

He tried to distract himself by looking out the window. He looked at the sky above and found the clouds imitating his feelings. They too appeared ready to burst at any moment.

However hard he tried, he was unable to forget her face and the yearning in those eyes— the eyes that spoke many stories without a word being said.

He tried to recall and relive every moment he'd spent with her during the past two weeks.

The first morning he came in was very

special.

She had stayed awake the whole night for him, and when he arrived, she had hugged him and spent the next several minutes touching and feeling every part of his face.

Whenever they were together, she held his hand, and when she slept, she only held them tighter. They played games, only for him to lose them all just so he could see her smile.

When he'd gotten the message about this mission, he steeled his heart and told her that he had to leave early.

He had known the things she had planned to do with him every day. After all, it had been a long wait for both of them: over two years. Yet she did not cry a bit when he broke the news.

Vaughn knew it wasn't going to be easy when he decided to join the army and serve the nation many years back. He believed then and still believed now that it was his life's purpose. To serve his country meant a lot to him. While a decision to turn back and head home was a very simple one, he knew he couldn't do that without fully failing himself. There was no looking back.

As the bus passed through the countryside, Vaughn saw a huge, colorful tulip farm on either side of the road.

The flowers smiled in the wind, paying no

heed to the otherwise gloomy weather.

Vaughn took the photo of his seven-year-old daughter out of his wallet. He gave her a kiss and promised that he would be back soon to spend the rest of the vacation with her.

Vaughn felt the first tear fall on his cheek. He wiped the drop, picked up his journal, and completed the poem as the bus neared its destination.

Living those promises that I'll never be able to share
For those victories that none might ever care
Like that tulip that smiles on a rainy day
I chose to bloom amid all gloom.

ABOUT THE AUTHOR

Little did Ramaswami know two moments would influence and define who he would later become. The first moment was when he wrote his first computer program, and the other was when he wrote his first extempore poem. While the joy of creating something new gave birth to a techie, a silent writer was born out of the curiosity to understand that very creation. Over the past twenty years, the writer and the techie grew together to inspire, contrast with, and even contradict one another. *In Few Words* is the writer's bold attempt to seize his identity completely. Born and raised in Chennai, India, Ramaswami currently lives with his family in the beautiful city of Redmond, Washington.

www.ingramcontent.com/pod-product-compliance
Lightning Source LLC
Chambersburg PA
CBHW021121130626
46554CB00002B/807